SEARCHING FOR LAURA INGALLS
A Reader's Journey

by Kathryn Lasky and Meribah Knight • photographs by Christopher G. Knight

ALADDIN PAPERBACKS

First Aladdin Paperbacks edition June 1998

Text copyright © 1993 by Kathryn Lasky and Meribah Knight
Photographs copyright © 1993 by Christopher G. Knight

Aladdin Paperbacks
An imprint of Simon & Schuster Children's Publishing Division
1230 Avenue of the Americas
New York, NY 10020

The text of this book was set in 14 pt. Garamond No. 3.
Printed and bound in the United States of America
10 9 8 7 6 5 4 3 2 1

The Library of Congress has cataloged the hardcover edition as follows:
Lasky, Kathryn. Searching for Laura Ingalls : a reader's journey / by Kathryn Lasky and
Meribah Knight ; photographs by Christopher G. Knight. — 1st ed.
p.   cm.
Summary: A young girl's fascination with Laura Ingalls Wilder's "Little House" books
leads her family on a trip to see some of the places featured in them.
ISBN 0-02-751666-0 (hc)
1. Wilder, Laura Ingalls, 1867-1957—Homes and haunts—Juvenile literature. 2.
Authors, American—20th century—Biography—Juvenile literature. 3. Frontier and
pioneer life—United States—Juvenile literature. [1. Wilder, Laura Ingalls, 1867-1957. 2.
Authors, American. 3. Frontier and pioneer life. 4. Voyages and travels.] I. Knight,
Meribah. II. Knight, Christopher G., ill. III. Title.
PS3545.I342Z76   1993   813'.52—dc20   92-26188
ISBN 0-689-82029-1 (pbk)

For Laura readers everywhere

—K.L. and C.G.K.

One

On her fifth birthday there was a box wrapped in blue paper with a silver ribbon. It was heavy, and when she unwrapped it and slid off the close-fitting top, she saw eight books with pale yellow covers all lined up inside. They were called the *Little House* books and they were all written by the same author—Laura Ingalls Wilder. The books told the true story of her life growing up on the prairie over one hundred years ago.

Meribah Knight was born 115 years after Laura Ingalls Wilder. Laura and Meribah never even lived on the planet earth at the same time. But that didn't matter. It didn't even matter that at five years old Meribah could not really read yet. She still wanted to read the stories of Laura.

The worlds of the two girls could not have been more different. Meribah lived in a city on the East Coast, and during the summer, right around the time of her birthday, her family always went to an island off the coast of Maine.

They began to read the first book that night on the island.

It was a night full of heavy warm air and wild winds. There was talk of a hurricane named Gloria chasing up the eastern seaboard. Meribah's father had gotten out shutters to put over the windows and had dragged the rowboat and the canoe out of the water and into a shed. But Meribah and her mom sat on the couch reading about Laura Ingalls, who was just a year younger at that time than Meribah and who was living in a little house in the big woods of Wisconsin.

The gale winds outside the shingled island house suddenly became the howling of the wolves at night in the big woods. Meribah wished that, like Laura, she had a trundle bed that slid out from under her parents' big bed, where she could stay safe and cozy from the wolves or the hurricane or whatever screamed in the night. She yawned.

"Time for bed?" Her mother asked.

"No! One more chapter." So her mother read on—about how Laura's pa shot the bear that stole the pig, about churning butter and baking bread, about making candy from molasses on pans full of snow, about Pa playing his fiddle, and about the lonesome moan of the wind through the immense woods of Wisconsin.

And then the island house lights blew out, and Meribah helped her mom light the candles and the kerosene lamp they had ready. Meribah's father, who was listening to the marine weather forecast on his portable radio, said, "She's thirty miles off Point Judith." He was talking about the hurricane named Gloria, and not wolves in the big woods.

"Is that far from here?" Meribah asked.

"Well, not when she's coming at thirty-five miles an hour, but she could veer and spin off to sea. Don't worry, we're safe." And Meribah half expected her dad to call her Flutterbudget just the

way Pa had called Laura. "Time to go to bed, though. Can't read with the lights out."

"How about kerosene lamps? That's how Laura's mom read to her. One more chapter, please!"

That night when they finally went to bed, Meribah's parents let her sleep at the foot of their bed in a sleeping bag. She was thinking about the wolf voices in the wind and what it would be like to try to cuddle a corncob doll like the one that Laura had. And she was wondering if there was still such a big woods. Her mom said that Laura was real. She was certainly the most real person Meribah had ever met up with in a book. But it was hard to imagine a woods so big that you traveled for a day, or a week, or a whole month, and there was still nothing but woods. That was what Laura Ingalls Wilder had written on the very first page of the first book.

"How far, Mom," Meribah asked, "would you have to go to find the big woods today?" But she could tell from their breathing that both her parents were sound asleep.

The wind rattled their house until Meribah thought every shingle would fall off, but Gloria never came. The hurricane spun inland near Portland after knocking some boats around and tearing up some trees. By the time the weather people were talking about the next hurricane—Herbie—Meribah and her mom had finished *Little House in the Big Woods* and were halfway through *Little House on the Prairie*.

Two

It is way past her bedtime, but Meribah is still up. Her light is off, but her flashlight is on under the covers. She is rereading her favorite part of *These Happy Golden Years*, the eighth and last of the *Little House* books, the one in which Laura gets married. It's the part just before her wedding, when Pa brings her a trunk to pack up her things for her new life with Almanzo. This is a happy-sad book. Meribah loves the part where Almanzo and Laura go buggy riding around a lake, and when they fall in love and when he asks her to marry him. But the leaving home part is so hard, especially when on the day before her wedding she sits on the doorstep and listens to Pa play the fiddle for the last time. Meribah reaches for her diary. It is so bright outside with the full moon and all the snow that she hardly needs the flashlight. There is a very bright streetlight just outside her window. So she creeps over to the window seat and opens the shutters.

This is the diary her mom bought her for their trip this summer. They are going to go to the prairie to see the places where Laura really lived. Her mom says they are still there, just different. There is still a Plum Creek, and there is a place called Pepin where the big woods were, and the little town on the prairie called De Smet is still there. They will even go look for Silver Lake. They will go in exactly 122 days, and she will take this diary and write all about it. She can't wait to start, so she starts the story now, this very minute, on a creaking cold night in Cambridge, Massachusetts, with the streetlights and moonlight turning her page bright. She is just learning how to write cursive. She should use cursive in her diary, she decides. It feels more important to write something in cursive.

CHAPTER ONE

Tomorrow at one o'clock in the afternoon I am going to be Laura. It's biography day in school. Sarah Jane is going to be Lillian Gish, a famous actress, and Nicole is going to be Benjamin Franklin and Zoe is going to be Napoleon, but I am going to be Laura Ingalls Wilder . . . and tell all about it.

The next day finally came. Biography day. In addition to Lillian Gish and Ben Franklin and Napoleon, there was one John Kennedy, one Martin Luther King, one Harriet Tubman, one Daniel Boone, one George Washington, one Larry Bird, and one Kit Carson. But there were three Laura Ingalls Wilders—Meribah, and her friends Zora and Abigail.

When it was time, we got our petticoats and our hoops on. I felt kind of itchy in my dress. I imagined how it felt to be Laura and wear an itchy dress like this every day. Back in the olden days girls always had to wear dresses. No pants for girls. They had the heat up too high in the school. That made it worse. So I kept thinking about being itchy all while I gave my report. And when I got home I thought what it would be like if Laura came to our class and saw me and Abigail and Zora dressed up like her and giving reports about her. I wondered what she would think of our time instead of the 1800s.

In the Long Winter it was never too hot, so maybe they weren't itchy. When they ran out of wood they had to twist hay and burn it to keep warm. Now that doesn't happen because we don't have as hard winters as they did back in the 1800s. It might be because the rain forests weren't being cut down as much. Laura might not have ever heard of the rain forest. We're learning about it now in third grade.

Meribah stopped writing. She had to think a minute about the rain forest and the big woods. Which was bigger? She'd have to ask her mom. But in just 121 days she would find out for herself!

Three

hrough the rest of the winter and the spring she counted the days. Her mom and dad
bought maps, road maps of Wisconsin and Minnesota and South Dakota. With an orange
felt-tipped pen they marked a route that they would follow. It was becoming more real all the
time. She could find the names on the map—De Smet and Walnut Grove and Pepin. She
could not find Plum Creek, and this worried her. Maybe it was just a little trickle of a creek
and too small to show up on a map. There were numbered roads and highways that led to all
of the other places. She would get there soon.

She started packing almost a week before they left. She packed and unpacked her bag at
least ten times. She had lists of things to bring. She would check them off and then put them
into her suitcase. Then she would unpack it and repack it all over. At first she packed all
eight of the *Little House* books. But her suitcase was too heavy. So then she decided to just
pack those books that took place in South Dakota, Minnesota, and Wisconsin because that
was where they were going. Finally on the night before they left she packed her suitcase for
the last time. She put in her sneakers and her shorts because it would be hot on the prairie
and she thought how lucky it was that little girls didn't have to wear long dresses, petticoats,
and high boots now. She packed her hair ribbons, just like Laura's, that her own mom had
bought her. She packed a calico skirt and blouse that looked a little bit old-fashioned but
wasn't hot. And of course her diary.

The next morning they drove to the airport and flew to Minnesota. They picked up their
"prairie schooner," but there were no Pet and Patty to pull the wagon and no dog named Jack

to chase behind, and even though her parents call it a prairie schooner, Meribah knew that it was a big old house on wheels, glaring with metal and humming with the mechanical horse-power of a gasoline engine.

There is a sign on the camper's side that says Cruise America, so Meribah's family decides that must be its name and calls it that. It has beds, closets, sinks, a microwave, and an air conditioner. Her dad says Cruise America is a gas guzzler and her mom thinks it's about the ugliest thing she has ever seen, but for the next ten days Cruise America will be their home. Meribah loves it. She loves the big windows that let her see the clouds in the biggest sky she's ever seen. She likes the air-conditioning and the refrigerator that her mom has packed with soda pop and Popsicles.

"This is the way to go!" She sighs, takes out her diary, and tries not to drip Popsicle juice on the pages.

Her mom is having fits all the way out of downtown Minneapolis. "You're hogging the road, Chris," she shouts to Meribah's dad.

"We *are* a hog—get used to it!" Her dad has never driven anything this big. He seems a little bit nervous.

Her older brother, Max, is reading a book called *Flattened Fauna: A Guide to Road-Killed Animals*.

"I bet we flatten a lot of fauna with this thing," Max says.

"Don't be gross!" Meribah snaps.

"They probably didn't have road kills back in Laura's time—nothing went fast enough. Keep your eyes peeled—"

"Don't use that expression, Max. I hate it," squeals Meribah.

"Okay, keep a sharp lookout for a *Bufo americanus*."

"What's that?" asked their mother.

"American toad, or road toad, and it says here that when they get run over—"

"Oh, Mom, he is so gross!"

"—a forelimb is extended as if the toad were waving good-bye."

"You are gross and mean," Meribah shouts.

The children start arguing. Meribah's mother wonders if Laura Ingalls Wilder left out the parts about the kids fighting in the back of the wagon and thinks that even when the backseat is ten feet away, it is still very annoying.

Meribah tries to write in her diary. The road is too bumpy and her handwriting looks rotten. She switches to print.

CHAPTER TWO

My brother is gross and horrible, and I wish he were a flattened fauna and that Mary and Laura were here instead of him. . . .

It is three hours later. Max has seen a smashed painted turtle and one skunk, and I saw a snake all smushed, and there are hardly any trees anyplace, and I can't believe there is going to be a big woods. . . .

Four

She came to find the big woods. There were miles of neatly plowed fields, some green, some russet, some tan, growing barley and corn and wheat. There were grain elevators and silos and miles and miles of railroad tracks. There were fences and farmhouses and big tractors and combines, but there was hardly a tree. Then suddenly they spotted row upon row of stiff little perfect evergreens all lined up as if they were ready to march, or maybe square dance. They stopped.

"Is this it?" Meribah said, stepping out of Cruise America.

Well, now the big woods hardly exists anymore because there are only seventy trees. I counted them. Mom says it must be a Christmas-tree farm. There are no more big woods because they cut them down for houses and furniture and to make farm fields for growing food out here. They've tried to plant some of the trees back, but there isn't enough room with all the farms and the fields.

I wonder how nice it would be to live here back in the 1800s when Laura did. In this new little woods I saw a monarch butterfly, but no bears or panthers—just butterflies and grasshoppers. The little woods is in a field all blowy with white flowers. It's hard to get scared in this woods.

Meribah thinks of that other woods, where the lonesome wind moaned and the darkness slid with the shadows of panthers and bears.

Five

The Little House in the Big Woods covers the period of Laura's life in Wisconsin, near Pepin, between the years 1871 and 1873. The Ingallses lived there on their small farm in the dense Wisconsin woods. There were not any big fields for growing big crops, but there were animals to hunt in the forests and fish to catch in the nearby streams and lakes.

One hundred and twenty-five years ago there was no road that led to the little house in the big woods of Wisconsin where Laura and her sisters Mary and Carrie were born, but now Highway 183 leads directly to it. There are signs along the highway to point the way and mark the miles to the Little House. At a wayside several hundred feet from the road there is a replica of the house where Laura and Mary lived.

But things have changed. There used to be two big oak trees where Pa would hang up the deer he'd hunted, to keep the meat safe from the bears. There had also been a section cut from a hollow tree, with nails driven through it, a little door with hinges, and a roof. He would hang the meat in this hollow old tree trunk, then build a small fire with hickory chips, shut the door, and smoke the meat. There had been a vegetable garden behind the little house. But had there been a lawn with grass? Meribah tried to remember. She remembered how Laura and Mary played catch with a pig's bladder. Had they run across beautiful green grass? That was what was there now.

The oak trees were gone, and so was the smokehouse. There was no vegetable garden or chopping block where Pa had cut wood. Now there was this beautiful green lawn, the kind her mom and dad were always trying to grow but never could. And right smack in the middle was a big flagpole with an American flag flying, and there were picnic tables and big trash cans that said Please Don't Litter. There was a historical marker with a bunch of words written in raised bronze letters that told about how important Laura Ingalls Wilder and this place were and how much she was loved and her delightful writing style, but Meribah got bored reading all those shiny bronze letters, and for a minute or more she felt very far from the book and the story.

She was about to wonder if any of it was real when her brother said, "Of course, it's not real—it's a replica. It was built in 1976."

But the little house felt kind of real when she got inside. It was much smaller than she had ever imagined. There were just three rooms downstairs and she heard another tourist say, "Now is this where they hung the hams and the venison to dry. Did they have a back door in the book? I don't remember any mention of a back door."

Meribah looked up at the attic and tried to imagine it stuffed with corn and pumpkins and the wrapped-up smoked hams and all the good food for the long winter stored from the harvest. And she remembered the picture in the book of Laura and Mary playing house up there, sitting on the gigantic pumpkins with their dolls. In a very small voice she whispered to her mother, "They should have at least put some big pumpkins up there."

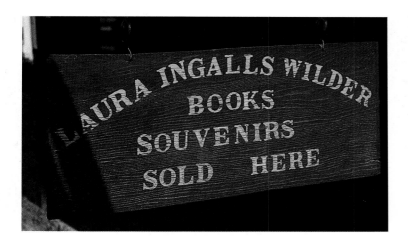

We went into the town of Pepin, just like Laura did in the book. This was a big deal for Laura. She had never been to a town, and it took them half the day to get there. It only took us fifteen minutes in Cruise America. Now there's a pizza parlor, two gas stations, and a beauty shop called Cut and Curl; I think that's a nice name for a beauty shop. There's a movie theater, Ralph's Bar, Mary's Kitchen (that's a restaurant), Dan's Grocery, and a historical museum. We went to it. They had old clothes from the time of Laura and Mary, and old trundle beds just like the kind she slept in, and they had quilts that had belonged to Laura. I saw old-fashioned dresses and shoes and stoves and grain cradles that were for putting grain into and an old apron that someone had worn.

They've got all this stuff for sale—there are Laura salt-and-pepper shakers and pot holders and little china bells and stationery and napkin rings and key chains and lots of books about Laura, not just ones that she's written but that people have written about her. I wonder what she'd think if she came back and saw all this stuff with her name on it. They even have a little cloth sack full of pebbles like the ones that Laura found at Lake Pepin when they went there for their picnic. She'd put so many in her pocket that they tore it right off her dress. . . .

They had a replica of the Charlotte doll that Laura got for Christmas, a real stuffed doll instead of the corncob doll. You could buy it. And Mom and I went halvesies on it.

We went to Lake Pepin right after the historical museum. We went swimming and had a snack on the beach. A couple of things are different now. In the book Mrs. Wilder said the lake was narrow, but now it's wide. It's a bulge in the Mississippi River, and it is so round that it looks like a big lake. They made it this way by building a big dam. And the second thing is about Indians. Back in Laura's time they were scared of Indians, but when I went there we saw white kids playing with Native American kids. They were playing water games. Laura and Mary's mom would never have let them do this. She was real scared of Indians. She probably would have thought they'd drown her daughters. My mom said I should go out there and play with them, but I was shy, not scared. They were almost teenagers! I found stones, like Laura's, and I found a plastic champagne cork and lots of metal pieces from soda pop cans.

Maybe, Meribah was thinking, these were the same stones that Laura picked up and put back. Maybe the stones weren't pretty enough back then. Maybe they hadn't been polished long enough by the years of water and wind rubbing them. Maybe the stones had to wait 125 years to get smooth and beautiful. And maybe if Laura came back today she would pick one up that she had thrown away before and think it was pretty enough to keep.

Six

In 1873 the Ingalls family sold their farm in Wisconsin and set out in their covered wagon to the western prairie of Minnesota. Laura was six and Mary was eight. They first lived in a dugout house on the banks of Plum Creek, two miles north of Walnut Grove.

The creek was Laura's whole world. It was her playground, her favorite place to be. It was where she tested herself and dared herself to do things that were unimaginable and sometimes naughty. It was at the creek that she nearly drowned one day when she disobeyed Pa and went by herself to the footbridge. She had gone there just to dip her feet in the water from the bridge. But the water was high and the current was stronger than she thought. It grabbed at her and nearly pulled her into the roaring creek. And she didn't know how to swim! She might have drowned.

Her father had taken her once to the deep, cool pool in the shade of the tall willows. They had waded into the water with all their clothes on. Her father had helped her and held her up in the water. She had always wanted to go back, but it was strictly forbidden. So for the most part Laura had to content herself with wading in the creek when the water was low and the current not too strong.

But Meribah could swim, and if there was one thing she wanted to do more than anything else, ever since she had read *On the Banks of Plum Creek*, the fourth book in the series, it was to swim in that very same creek where Laura had waded. And to do it in her clothes. She had even picked out the skirt. It was the special one that she had packed, pink calico with a matching blouse. She had it all planned out.

But before they got to the creek there was another museum, with a replica of a covered wagon, just like the one the Ingallses traveled in, and a schoolhouse just like the one where Laura and Mary went to school.

Well, I like Cruise America better than this covered wagon, I'll tell you that right now. We went inside the old schoolhouse. It had only six desks and one for someone who was bad and one for the teacher.

The creek looks almost the same as it did when Laura played on its banks, but there are beautiful cornfields as far as you can see all around. The dugout house caved in long ago, and is now just an indentation in the bank.

I finally had my dream come true, but it was almost a bad dream, a nightmare. I got to go wading and swimming in Plum Creek.

It was warm and the current in the creek was going really fast. When I waded into the water I fell, but I got used to it and started to swim. When I stood up my clothes were heavy and wet. I felt like stones were hanging on my skirt. I climbed trees that were sticking out over the creek.

I remembered in the book how Laura went to look under branches and rocks for the old crab, the one she used to scare Nellie Oleson, the stuck-up girl in the book. I looked for it, too. I couldn't find it, so I swam along some more and hung from branches.

But guess what? When I came out of Plum Creek I saw this thing that looked like a glob of mud on my foot, and then I thought, It's a black slug, but then I thought, Slugs aren't black. Then I remembered. It came back all awful. It was a leech just like the ones Laura got on her. I had forgotten this whole part of the book, the part about the leeches. My stomach flip-flopped, my brain went crazy, and I started to scream. Of course my dad just had to take a picture before he pulled it off me.

There wasn't any blood. But I was still waving my hands in the air screaming, even though I didn't have it on me anymore. When I got to the Cruise America I told my brother. He said they might be great-great-grand-leechie children of the ones that got on Laura. Then he left Cruise America because he's really scared of leeches and was worried I still had some on me, but I didn't. This was how scared I was: I was hyperventilating. My mom said so. She said, "Stop hyperventilating, Meribah!" I think she thought I might have a heart attack. But I didn't.

We left Plum Creek. I felt good enough to play on a haystack later that day on our way to De Smet, the little town on the prairie. I had always wanted to slide down a haystack. Laura did it. But the hay was kind of hard-feeling and I was worried that the farmer might see me and get mad. But there weren't any leeches.

Seven

The year 1879 was a hard one for the Ingalls family. In the spring they all became sick, but Laura's sister Mary was the sickest with what the doctors called brain fever. It left Mary blind, and Laura had to become her eyes. That summer the Ingallses made their last move, into the Dakota Territory. Pa's first job there was that of timekeeper and paymaster for the Chicago and Northwestern Railroad that was being built. In the beginning they lived in the railroad camps near Silver Lake, but their first winter was spent in the surveyors' house on Silver Lake near present-day De Smet, which was the railroad town. The following spring of 1880 the Ingalls family moved to their 160 acres of homestead land a mile from De Smet. To the north was Silver Lake, to the west was the Big Slough. Pa built a shanty as their first house and planted cottonwoods. The books *By the Shores of Silver Lake, Little Town on the Prairie, The Long Winter,* and *These Happy Golden Years* all took place in this region.

Meribah stood in the middle of the street. She could not believe that it could be this quiet and this empty. The blue sky stretched overhead and she felt as if she were the only one to see it. But it was the Fourth of July! Where were the people? Where was the music? The parade? Why, on the homestead one mile away, Laura and Mary had heard the booms as the blacksmith in town had exploded gunpowder under his anvil. Meribah remembered from the book that it was supposed to be the noise of the battles the Americans had fought for their independence. But now, more than one hundred years later, she was standing on the quietest street in the quietest town she had ever been in.

The stillness was so thick it made Meribah's skin itch. She squeezed her Charlotte doll, the one she had bought in the souvenir shop in Pepin, and tried to figure it out. They had gotten up so early to get here in time for the Fourth, and nothing was happening. Even her mom was disappointed. She went into the general store to check.

"Well?" Meribah asked.

"Well, I guess we've come about one hundred years too late—they don't celebrate it anymore."

"Why not?"

"I don't know," her mom said. "They just said people stay home in their air-conditioning or go down to a lake and go waterskiing."

"Silver Lake?"

"I don't think so. They say there's a big lake about forty miles from here."

Both Meribah and her mom now stood there and tried to imagine that time in the summer so long ago when Pa took Laura and her younger sister Carrie to the celebration in town. Ma had made sandwiches. Pa had blacked his boots. Laura and Carrie had worn their best calico dresses sprigged with flowers. The street had been crowded. There had been lots of noise as firecrackers exploded in booms and sizzles. Laura Ingalls Wilder had described how there were treats to be bought and a whole barrel of fresh lemonade with thick slices of lemon floating on the top. Then a man had gotten up and talked about freedom and cutting loose from the despots in Europe. It was the first time Meribah had ever heard the word *despot*. She had remembered thinking it was a cute little word for such a rotten person. The man didn't

make a long fancy speech. He just went on to re-cite the Declaration of Independence. "When in the course of human events. . . ." And the words had made Laura and Carrie feel solemn and glorious. She remembered reading that, and it had made Meribah feel solemn and glorious, too, when her dad had read that part of the book to her. But now she just felt hot and disappointed.

We visited the surveyors' house. Laura lived in it by Silver Lake, but somebody moved the whole house into town. It seemed small to me because now we live in bigger houses. The people that had lived there had been gone for a long time, but their furniture was there and there were still memories.

I saw the chest that Pa had carved for the girls' clothes. You could tell it was handmade from all the grooves. He must have enjoyed carving wood because you need a lot of patience for the piece of work he did. The handles were shaped like leaves and at the tip of the leaf there was a curl. I would like to keep my clothes in a chest like that.

On the chest was the book of poems that Ma had bought for Laura one Christmas and that Laura had accidentally discovered, so she had to pretend to be surprised on Christmas morning. I thought about Laura and her sisters making Christmas presents that winter in the surveyors' house—how Laura had made a necktie for her father and an apron for her mother, and she and her sister Mary had made the mittens for little Carrie. Then I remembered the whatnot—and there it was standing in the corner, just the way she had described it—a three-cornered cupboard with five shelves and all decorated with paper folded in complicated ways. The house didn't seem so lonely after all. It was still a cozy place to be.

Back in the air-conditioned comfort of Cruise America, they decided to go have a picnic at Silver Lake. Silver Lake was where Almanzo Wilder had taken Laura buggy riding during their courting days. And it was where the Ingallses had first lived when Pa was working on the railroad.

So they went to the lake for a picnic. But there was no lake.

"It's not funny!" Meribah growled in a low voice to her brother. They were standing where Silver Lake had once been. A gate led into two very square, unnaturally green ponds. The sign announced that this was a sewage treatment area. Her brother was making gross sewage jokes. The rest of Silver Lake had disappeared when the water had been drained many years ago to make more farmland. But the railroad was still there.

Mom and Dad say it's got to be the very same one Laura's pa helped build. So we walked along it for almost a mile and I collected pieces that had fallen off—iron spikes and a curved C-shaped thing. Mom says that they're my first real souvenirs.

We went out to the place where Laura and Almanzo lived when they first got married, the claim where their daughter Rose was born. No one had been there for a long, long time, but a prairie dog had dug a hole where the house used to be, and in the dirt he brought up I found a piece of glass that might be from their house. It was silvery, which means it has been in a fire. That's what my dad said. And Laura had survived a fire there. So it might be from that fire. There were frogs hopping around in the tall grass, too. So we tried to catch one, me and Max.

Eight

On the south side of the bluff there is a windbreak of cottonwoods. To the west shafts of late afternoon sunlight turn the long grass of the Big Slough into fiery gold. This is the last place where the Ingallses all lived together as a family. When they first came out to this homestead, just one mile north of De Smet, there were no trees at all, except for one that was called the Lone Tree, but that stood miles away on the shore of Lake Henry. From its seeds little trees eventually started to grow, and Pa had brought five seedlings to their new homestead, one for each member of his family—Ma and the four girls. Now the trees are all that is left. They stand immense, casting dappled shadows over the tall grass, their lower branches gently arching, just right for hanging a rope swing, or maybe even holding a small tree house.

Meribah walks under the shade of the five cottonwoods. The silky fluff from their blossoms tumbles on whispers of wind across the grass. There are groves of trees in the distance now, and fields and farms and a big highway, but there is still the emptiness, too. More emptiness than she has ever seen. The enormous silence of the prairie swells up around her. She remembers the terrible time when Grace, the baby sister of the three Ingalls girls, got lost on this prairie. How terrified Laura had been. How they had searched and how Laura was the one to find the baby playing happily in a buffalo wallow.

"I wonder if I could find a buffalo wallow, Mom?" Meribah asks. Her mom's not sure. The buffalo have been gone for so many years. But Meribah remembers that even back in Laura's time they had been gone for a while. The wallow was a place in the ground that the buffalo would paw up and then wallow about in the dust. When Laura found Grace, the old wallow was blooming with violets and aflutter with butterflies. It looked so beautiful with the flowers and her baby sister playing in its center that Laura thought she had found a fairy ring.

The buffalo might be gone, and the lost sister long ago found, but was it possible maybe to find the dim impression of an old wallow and for just a minute, and not a second longer, to taste right in the back of her throat the horrible panic that Laura must have felt, and then to see a fairy ring? She looked and looked. The prairie rolled off into the distance in gentle swells. She picked up some of the fluff from the cottonwoods Pa had planted and held it for a long time in her hand. She thought about the iron spike she had found from the railroad he had built and the piece of silvery glass in her pocket that had been through the fire. She

thought about all these little pieces of an almost vanished world and about how all the things that the Ingallses had built with their hands had disappeared, but that the trees had finally grown up and were big enough for children to play in. Then she thought about how if she were Laura, come back with her sisters, she would describe this place to her blind sister, Mary, 110 years later.

This is what I would say:
The cottonwoods are still here, all five of them. And they are very big.
There's a plaque on a rock that talks all about us.
The path is still here.
The Big Slough is still here, and there's a big barn across from it on the other side.
The buffalo wallow isn't there anymore. I couldn't find it.
The town is still here, and the street has pavement, and there are cars and people.
There are more people than you can think of, but there weren't many on the Fourth of July and they
*   didn't have any celebration.*
There are houses, many more houses than before.
And even though there are trees, the sky still looks so big. . . .

And there is a little girl sitting on a rock just up the slope from the cottonwoods, and she doesn't look at all like us. Her legs are bare and she's wearing these funny short pants, but I think that she might be waiting for us.